# Bailey and the Bear

## (A Book About Anger Management)

written by
**Holly Duhig**

Illustrated by
**Drue Rintoul**

HEALTHY MINDS

# BookLife
## PUBLISHING

©2019
**BookLife Publishing
King's Lynn
Norfolk PE30 4LS**

A catalogue record for this
book is available from the
British Library.

**ISBN:** 978-1-78637-360-1

**Written by:**
Holly Duhig

**Edited by:**
Kirsty Holmes

**Designed & Illustrated by:**
Drue Rintoul

With grateful thanks to Place2Be for their endorsement of this series.

**These titles have been developed to support teachers and
school counsellors in exploring pupils' mental health, and have
been reviewed and approved by the clinical team at Place2Be,
the leading national children's mental health charity.**

Bailey has a problem: a big bear-sized problem. Bailey's bear follows her everywhere. He's there when she wakes up and there when she goes to bed at night. Bear makes Bailey feel very grouchy.

Bailey has been feeling more and more grouchy lately – especially when her older brother, Jason, is around.

Jason is three whole years older than Bailey and he's better than her at everything!

He beats her at video games...

...he gets better school reports...

...and he even beats her at football!

Worst of all, Jason gets all the attention from Mum. Bailey just gets shouted at.

Bailey's bear was small at first, almost like a teddy bear. When Bear was with her, Bailey felt brave and she had a big **ROAR**. She used it to scare her brother away, but it got her in trouble sometimes too.

Now Bailey's bear is much bigger. When Bailey walks around the house, Bear climbs onto her back. He is very heavy and he makes Bailey stomp, stomp, stomp down the stairs.

"Stop stomping!" shouts Bailey's mum. Bailey doesn't know how to tell her that it's her grumpy bear making her footsteps loud.

7

Bailey doesn't want to take her bear to school today. She has football practice before lunch and Bear is not very calm at football. Bears don't need to go to school. They are used to living in the wild where there is lots of space and no teachers and certainly no rules.

"Don't forget your PE kit!" yells Bailey's mum.

Bear always sits next to Bailey in the classroom, which means that her friend Lucy doesn't want to sit next to her anymore. Bear has been known to growl at Lucy when she asks to borrow a pencil or a ruler.

"Bears don't share," says Bear to Bailey. Bear makes Bailey feel quite lonely sometimes.

Bailey wants to sit still and listen to her teacher, Mr Green, but Bear is getting on her nerves. Bears are too big for classrooms. They get grumpy and fidgety. "Bears don't like chairs!" Bear grumbles.

Someone is tapping a pencil loudly behind Bailey and it all feels too much. She growls and slams her fists on the table.

"What is the answer to my question Bailey?" booms Mr Green. Bailey hasn't been listening. "Thirteen?" she guesses. Everyone laughs. Bailey turns bright red from embarrassment; her fists clench and she feels angrier than ever.

When it's time for football practice, Bailey is not in a good mood. Bailey is very good at football, but Bear wants to be part of the game today. He climbs up onto Bailey's back. It makes Bailey hot, bothered and out of breath.

When she misses a goal, Bear tells her to kick the goal post, but all it does is hurt her foot. When the other team score, Bear tells Bailey to shout bad words. "That's enough of that Bailey or you'll be sent off!" shouts Mr Green. Bailey wonders if he has a bear of his own.

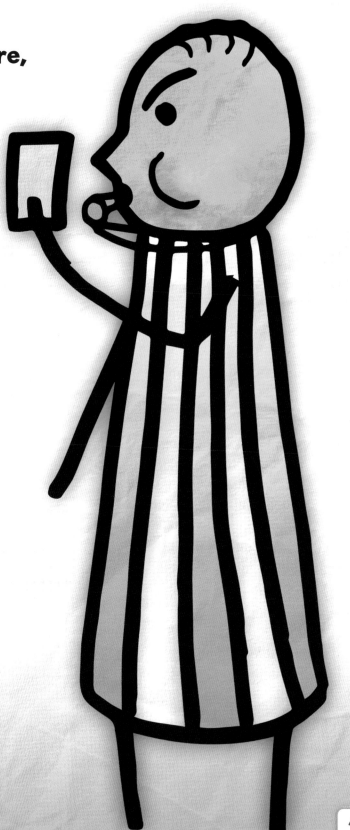
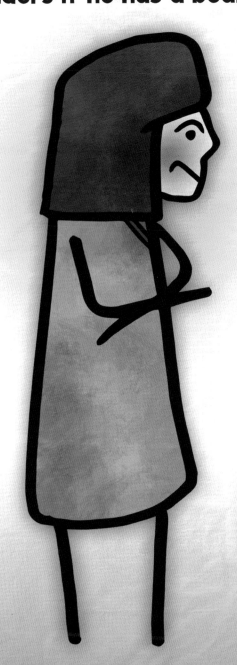

"Stop hogging the ball, Bailey," bellows Mr Green. Bailey hates being shouted at. Her cheeks go red, her fists clench and her legs turn to jelly. She wants to roar. Bear wants to roar too. "Bears don't share!" they roar together.

Suddenly, Lucy tackles the ball. Bailey falls over and it sends Bear flying backwards.

Bailey is furious. So is Bear. It feels like there is a red fog around her.

"Run after her!" roars Bear. Bailey runs, and runs, and runs, until...

WHACK! Bailey kicks Lucy in the back of the legs. Really hard.

"**AGHHHH!**" shouts Lucy.

"**SCHEEEECH!**" goes Mr Green's whistle.

"**Uh oh,**" says Bailey.

Mr Green shows Bailey a red card and gives her a detention.

Bailey hates detention. She's not angry anymore and she wishes she could say sorry to Lucy. Bear doesn't want to apologise. "Bears don't care," he grumps.

But Bailey does care. She thinks about having to tell her mum about the detention. She will probably get shouted at and Jason will look smug.

Just then, Bailey starts to cry. Mr Green rushes over. "What's the matter, Bailey?" he asks as he hands her a spotty handkerchief.

Bailey tells Mr Green all about her grumpy bear and how angry he makes her. She tells him about Mum and Jason too.

Mr Green asks Bailey if she would like to go to see the school counsellor. "She is really very good. She helped me tame my own angry bear once when class 2A were getting out of hand. Should we take your bear to see her?"

The school counsellor's name is Sam. Sam says that lots of people have a bear and Bailey is not alone. "Bears need to be angry," she explains. "It's how they survive in the wild. But school isn't the wild."

Bailey tells her about the football match and, to her surprise, Sam is very understanding.

Sam says everyone needs a bear around sometimes to remind them to stand up for themselves. "Bears can be dangerous if you always let them have their way, though. You need to be their referee!"

Bailey thinks that this is something she could do. After all, she's very good at football.

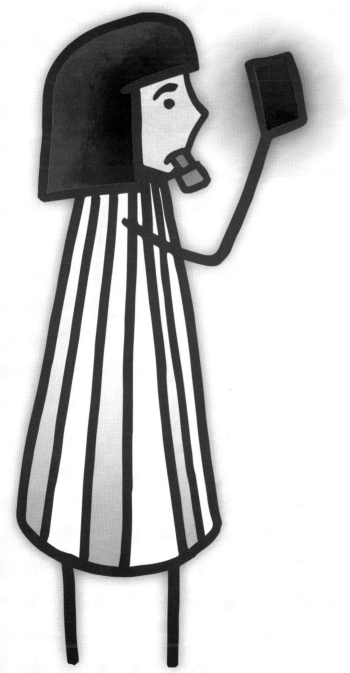
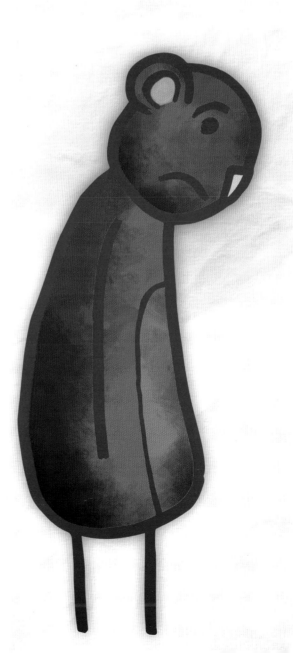

Sam helps Bailey make a yellow card and a red card with scissors and crayons that she can show Bear when he's getting out of control.

"Did you know that bears can hibernate, Bailey?" asks Sam. "It means that they can sleep for a long, long time, and your bear looks like he needs it."

Bailey thinks hibernation sounds like a good idea. Sam teaches Bailey how to send Bear to sleep by taking a few deep breaths and counting down from ten when he is getting too much to handle.

Bailey thinks it might take a while for Bear to fully hibernate but, in the meantime, she has Sam, the handy bear handler!

# More Information

Everyone feels angry from time to time. But when someone feels angry a lot of the time and it is affecting their own wellbeing, or the wellbeing of other people, it might be because of a problem with anger management. Anger is a complicated emotion and is often the result of other emotions such as embarrassment, jealousy, stress or hurt. It can also be the sign of a mental health condition.

If you are struggling with anger, it is important to talk to someone you trust - such as a doctor, counsellor, parent or carer. Talking about your anger, as well as other emotions, is the first step to feeling better.